CUENTO
DE LUZ

To all of the friends who hug cypresses.

- Marta Sanmamed -

Text © Marta Sanmamed
Illustrations © Sonja Wimmer
This edition © 2014 Cuento de Luz SL
Calle Claveles 10 | Urb Monteclaro | Pozuelo de Alarcón | 28223 | Madrid | Spain
www.cuentodeluz.com
Title in Spanish: Cipariso
English translation by Jon Brokenbrow

ISBN: 978-84-16147-10-6

Printed by Shanghai Chenxi Printing Co., Ltd. August 2014, print number 1454-2

FSC
www.fsc.org
MIX
Paper from
responsible sources
FSC® C007923

CYPARISSUS

That which dies is never forgotten; that which is forgotten, dies

Marta Sanmamed & Sonja Wimmer

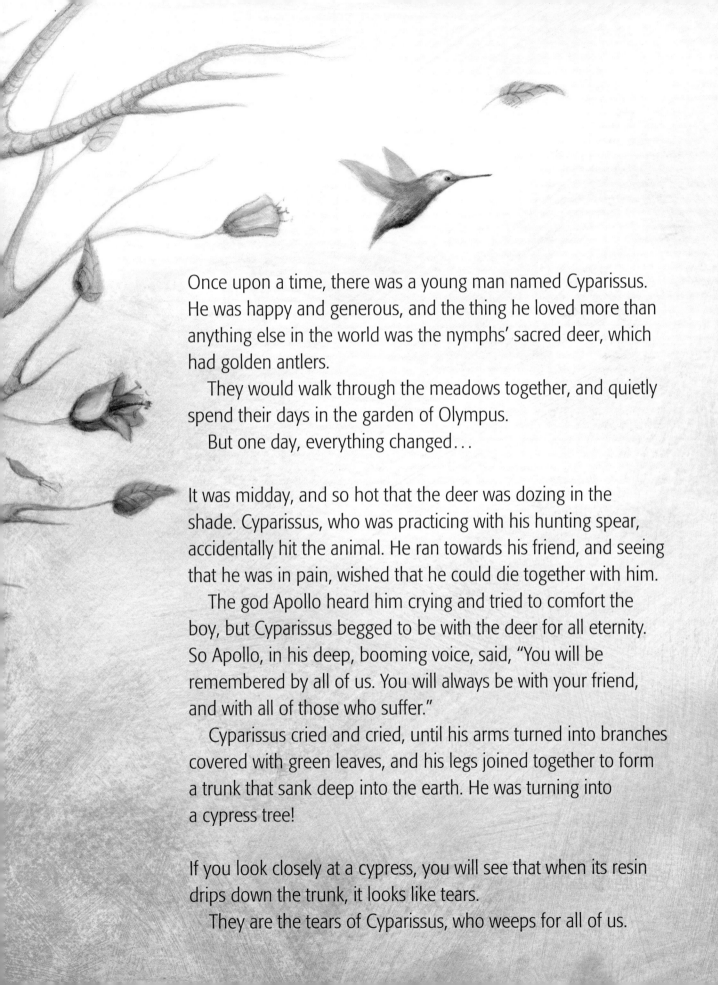

Once upon a time, there was a young man named Cyparissus.
He was happy and generous, and the thing he loved more than
anything else in the world was the nymphs' sacred deer, which
had golden antlers.

They would walk through the meadows together, and quietly
spend their days in the garden of Olympus.

But one day, everything changed…

It was midday, and so hot that the deer was dozing in the
shade. Cyparissus, who was practicing with his hunting spear,
accidentally hit the animal. He ran towards his friend, and seeing
that he was in pain, wished that he could die together with him.

The god Apollo heard him crying and tried to comfort the
boy, but Cyparissus begged to be with the deer for all eternity.
So Apollo, in his deep, booming voice, said, "You will be
remembered by all of us. You will always be with your friend,
and with all of those who suffer."

Cyparissus cried and cried, until his arms turned into branches
covered with green leaves, and his legs joined together to form
a trunk that sank deep into the earth. He was turning into
a cypress tree!

If you look closely at a cypress, you will see that when its resin
drips down the trunk, it looks like tears.

They are the tears of Cyparissus, who weeps for all of us.

Irene and Lucy were inseparable. Lucy was fourteen, which is very old for a dog, but she still loved to go to the park and chase sticks, just like she did when she was a puppy.

But one day, everything changed…

When Irene arrived home from school, she couldn't find her friend anywhere.

She asked where Lucy was, and her mom told her that Lucy had run off in the park, that she was sure she wouldn't come back, and all that Irene could do was to be strong.

So that was what she did…

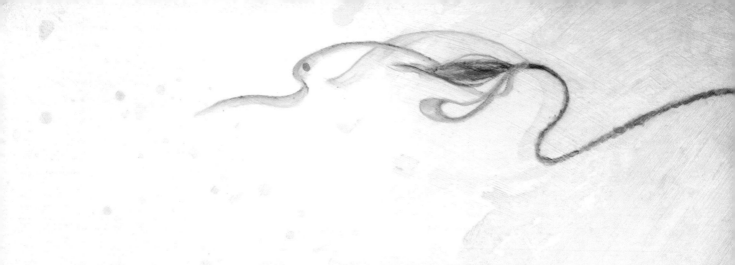

In her notebook, Irene wrote down all of the things she thought made people strong, and worked out a special routine: she roller-skated until her legs hurt, rode her bike until her muscles ached, jumped rope, ran up and down the stairs, and did push-ups.

And before going to bed, she would look in the mirror to see if she had gotten strong enough for Lucy to come home.

She trained and trained, but nothing happened.

Paddy was a very gentle horse, and he knew just how to behave with the children who came to riding class. His favorite rider was George, a little boy who rode on Saturdays. He was the only one who brought him green apples. Paddy didn't like red apples very much, or sugar cubes, but he ate them all the same, just to make people happy.

But one day, everything changed…

George looked into Paddy's stable one fall morning, and saw that it was empty.

He asked the owner of the stable where Paddy was. He pointed to the sky, and in a sad voice, said, "Paddy's up in the clouds."

George couldn't understand how a little horse could jump that high, but he decided he had to get everything ready for whenever he came back.

So that was what he did…

George spent the next few days wondering how Paddy had managed to get all the way up into the clouds. Had he used a gigantic ladder? Had he tied thousands of balloons around his belly? Had he traveled on a rocket?

He couldn't find an answer, but he was sure that his friend would soon be coming back. So, to stop him from bumping his head on the ground, George began to pile up all of the cushions and pillows he could find in his house.

He waited and waited, looking up at the sky, but nothing happened.

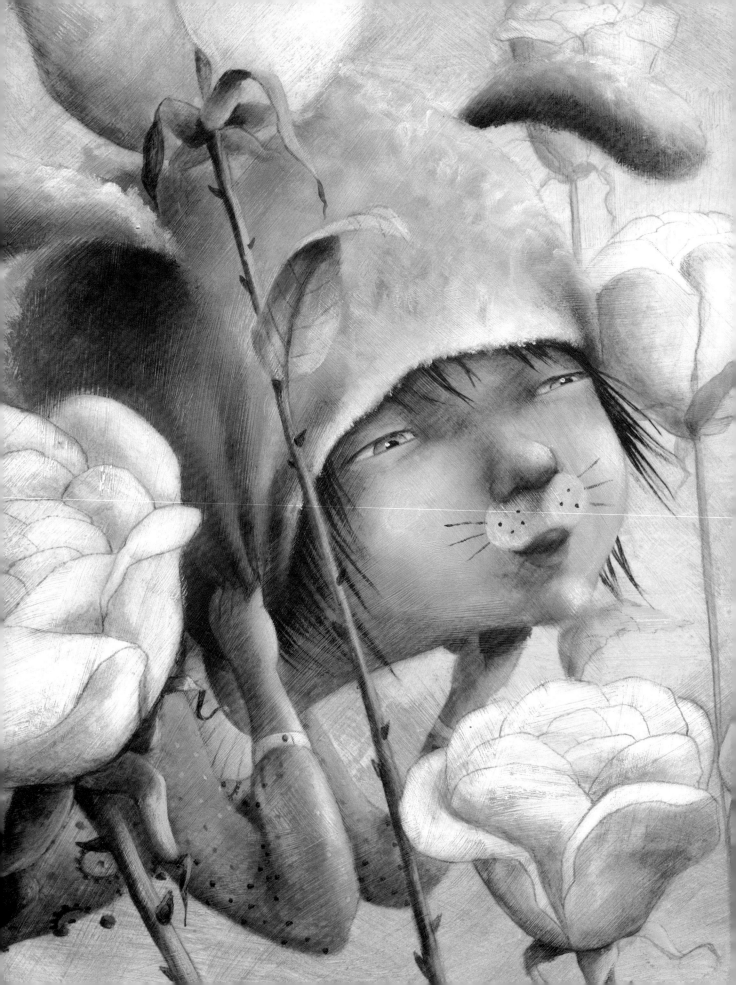

Gus was a gray rabbit who loved to eat corn. He hopped merrily around Molly's garden, and his favorite place was the flower bed full of white roses. He loved playing dress up and hide-and-go-seek, and having his tummy tickled.

But one day, everything changed…

Molly searched everywhere for her floppy-eared friend, but she couldn't find him.

She asked her daddy where Gus was, and he told her that her little rabbit was fast, fast asleep…

Molly thought that sleeping was something very bad, and decided to stay awake for the rest of her life, until Gus came back.

So that was what she did…

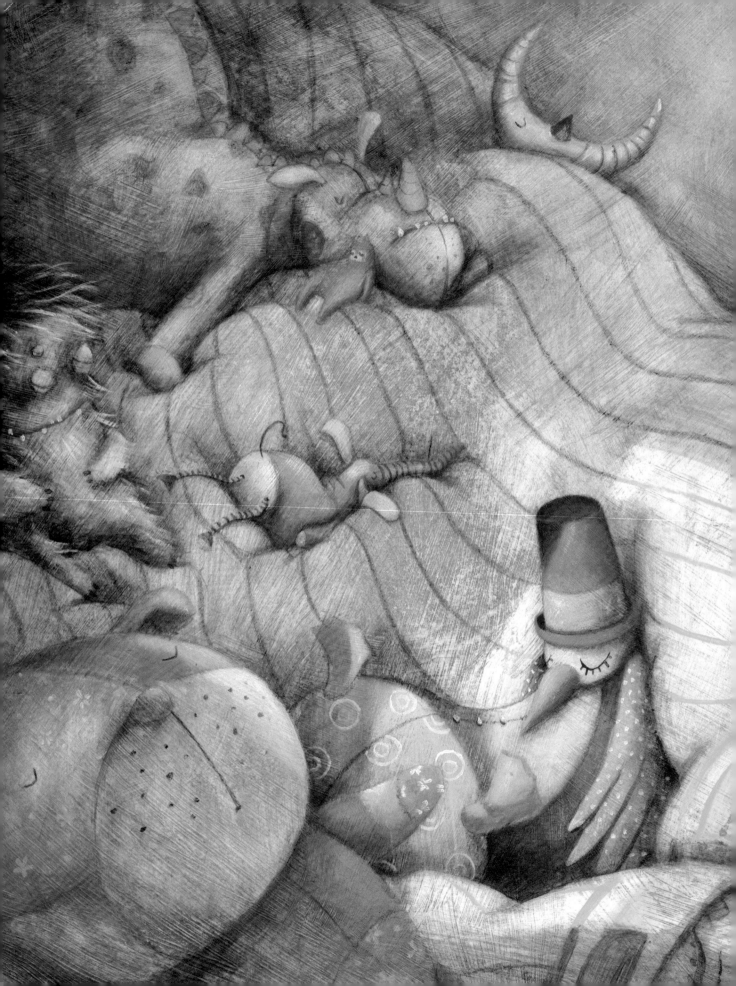

During the long, dark nights, Molly would be woken by nightmares every time she dozed off to sleep. Her tummy and her head began to ache just like when she had the flu, and she felt very, very tired. But she missed Gus so much that she wouldn't let herself rest for even a second, even when her cousins snuggled up with her in the big bed after a night of movies and popcorn.

She waited and waited, with her eyes wide, wide open, but nothing happened.

Tango was a happy little goldfinch who loved to sing. Danny's grandpa had named him, because he said he could sing tangos better than the legendary Gardel (a very famous singer whom Danny had never heard of). Tango loved to eat sunflower seeds and sing his songs from the windowsill.

But one day, everything changed…

Danny went to buy some bread, but when he came back, the house was silent.

He asked his grandpa what was wrong, and he told Danny that Tango had gone on a long, long journey…

Danny couldn't understand how his friend could have left without telling him! So he began to stuff his T-shirts into his backpack.

He had to go with him!

So that was what he did…

Danny took all of the coins out of his piggy bank and walked to the bus station. But when he asked how much a ticket to Argentina cost, he realized he didn't have enough

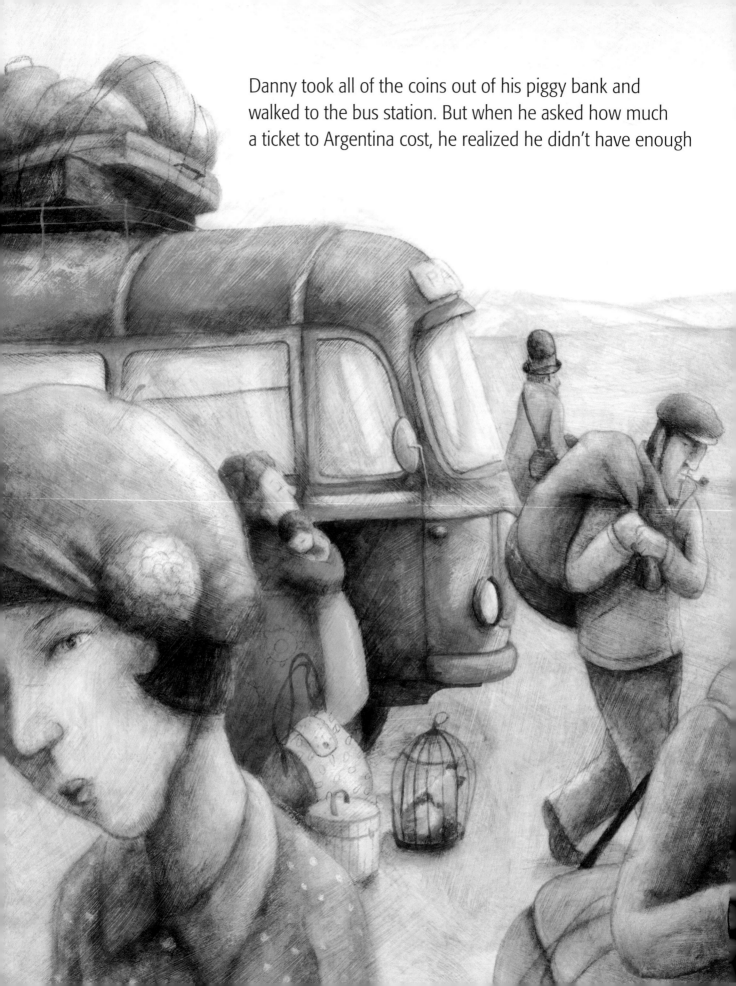

money for such a long journey. He sat glumly on a bench, expecting his friend to suddenly hop off one of the crowded buses that pulled in.

He waited and waited at the station, but nothing happened.

As Cyparissus was the tallest tree in the city, he had been watching the children for some time, and decided to help them. So he shook his branches, and called to the four winds.

The North Wind covered itself with feathers, turning into a happy little bird just like Tango.

The South Wind drew a pair of almond-shaped eyes in the clouds, just like Lucy's.

The East Wind shook its mane and galloped, whinnying, towards George's house.

And the West Wind grew a round, fluffy tail, just like Gus's, and set off towards Molly's house.

They all knew what Cyparissus needed, because they'd done it a million times before.

When the four winds found the children, they brought them together, and gently led them towards the park where Cyparissus was waiting for them.

Molly was scared of the big gate and the high walls, but George took her hand and squeezed it, and she felt much better. They soon realized they were entering a cemetery, but they weren't afraid. They confidently walked to each of the places the huge cypress tree pointed to with its long branches.

Cyparissus stretched and stretched to show the children the most important places in the cemetery.

They marveled at everything he showed them: stone angels, hourglasses, owls, butterflies, bats, flowers, and hearts carved next to names and dates. And they read the words that were written there: "We will never forget you" and "Forever in our hearts."

The children then understood that their friends had not set off on a long journey, they had not fallen asleep, and they had not gotten lost in the park. However hard they trained to be stronger, they would never, ever see them again, because, quite simply, they had died.

It hurt them to accept it, but Cyparissus pointed to a tombstone, on which was written the answer to all of their questions, an answer that filled them with hope:

"That which dies is never forgotten; that which is forgotten, dies."

The four friends put their arms around Cyparissus' trunk and hugged him tight, telling the tree about Paddy's green apples, about how Lucy loved to run around, about Gus's hiding places, and about Tango's beautiful songs.

They spent the afternoon chatting and telling stories, just as if they were around a campfire.

Sometimes they laughed, sometimes they cried, but they felt wonderful, because they had all found their friends where they had never looked for them before: *within their own hearts*.

Before heading home, the children decorated Cyparissus with the things that had belonged to their friends. Molly joined together Lucy and Gus's leashes, fastening them around the trunk to make a pretty belt. Danny hung Tango's cage in the branches so that another little bird could use it, and George decorated a branch with Paddy's bridle.

The four winds embraced them, and they all smiled together as they realized that precisely at that moment, the tallest tree in the whole city *had stopped crying*.